Billy Fustertag Learns Comedy

By

Brad Tassell

Illustrations by

Logan Sibrel

Llessat Publishing

Santa Claus, Indiana

For Janet, Brooke, Ashley,
Mathew, Aubrie, Allison, and Sam

Library of congress cataloging-in-publication
Printed by Abbey Press
50 Hill Drive
Saint Meinrad, IN 47577

ISBN 0-89708-226-5
Published by Llessat Publishing
PO Box 742
Santa Claus, IN 47579
For ordering information or school visits go to: www.billyfustertag.com

Billy Fustertag was funny.

All of his friends said so.

During recess he'd have all of his classmates cracking up. He could walk just like Principal Merryweather. He could talk like crabby old Mrs. Applehouse. He could mush up his face to look exactly like Mr. Crumblebean does when he hears any of what he calls, "Student shenanigans."

Billy was funny alright, and not just with impersonations. He could tell stories too. His whole family could tell you how hilarious it was when Billy told about the time Grandma left her teeth in the wrong cup and how surprised Grandpa was when his morning coffee looked like it was smiling at him.

Billy's cousin Suzy will tell you that she laughs so hard milk comes out of her nose when he tells her the story about his bald uncle.

Uncle Albert has one really long hair that he twirls around the top of his head to make it look like a full head of hair. Suzy laughs so hard that she cries when Billy pretends to wrap one long hair around his head and then tells her Uncle Albert's hair is growing out of Uncle Albert's ear.

Billy Fustertag was funny.

So, it was no surprise that when the Alfred P. Soffenburg Elementary School planned a talent show, Mr. Answerpenny came to Billy first to ask him if he would like to do a comedy routine.

"You bet I do!" said Billy. "I'll knock 'em dead."

"Well good, Billy," said Mr. Answerpenny. "I'll put you down as our main act. You'd better get to work on what you are going to say."

"Oh, don't worry about that," Billy laughed. "I'm so funny. I'll know what to say."

"Okay, Billy, we'll be counting on you." said Mr. Answerpenny.

For the next couple weeks all the kids who were going to be in the show worked on their acts.

Little Louise Guttelbach played her piano solo over and over. Ernie Kettlejabber practiced singing his song so many times he couldn't talk for a whole day. After that he sang his song more quietly so his voice would be ready. The Sanderpacket twins practiced their tap dancing so much you would swear there was only one tap-tap-tap on the floor even though they were both dancing.

Everyone was working very hard to prepare for the big talent show, except Billy that is. He wasn't worried. He knew that he was funny. Everyone knew. Why should he waste his time practicing? He did funny things all the time without even trying.

This picture was drawn by:

Ashley Kamuf
Grade 11

Mr. Answerpenny was not as sure as Billy.

"Billy, have you decided what stories you are going to tell?" asked Mr. Answerpenny.

"I've got plenty of stories." said Billy.

"Do you know what impressions you will do?" asked Mr. Answerpenny.

"It doesn't matter," Billy replied. "They're all funny."

The night of the first annual Alfred P. Soffenburg Talent Show was turning out to be very exciting when Mayor Jerrymanor showed up to run the cake walk for the Alfred P. Soffenburg Second Annual Carnival Day.

Tonight it seemed like the whole town was in the audience. Marvin "Big Dog" Enginecutter, the radio DJ from "All Hits" WCPK cowpoke radio, was sitting front and center. Melinda Quillinfeather, the newspaper lady who called the high school talent show "a stinkeroo," was pacing in the back of the theater. Alfie Gnomesitter, the television weatherman, was sitting just a few feet from the stage.

Backstage Mr. Answerpenny was making sure everybody was ready to go on.

Ernie was nervous, but sang, "Peep, Peep, Goes the Chick" better than ever.

One of the twins said she had a tummy ache before they went onstage. Mr. Answerpenny said they were just butterflies, and they would make her dance even better.

He was right!

Louise said she was really really scared about playing in front of so many people and asked Mr. Answerpenny if she could get some butterflies for her belly because the twins had danced so wonderfully.

Mr. Answerpenny said she didn't need any because of how long and hard she had worked on her piano song. Billy laughed because he didn't need butterflies to be funny.

"Okay Billy, you're next," said Mr. Answerpenny. "Break a leg." Mr. Answerpenny walked onstage as everyone was still clapping for Louise.

"Ladies and gentleman, we have saved the best for last. Let's have a big round of applause for the comedy of Billy Fustertag." Everybody started clapping, and Billy ran to the center of the stage.

When the applause died down, Billy was still standing onstage, but suddenly couldn't think of anything to say. He had a million stories, but he couldn't think of one of them. Who were the people he imitated so well? He couldn't remember. Suddenly, Billy felt hot and his stomach started to hurt. Maybe the butterflies would help him remember what he used to say that was funny. But it didn't help.

Billy just didn't say anything.

Some of the kids from his class started to laugh, but not in the way he liked. It was the kind of laughter that Big Peter Gompwither used when he knocked down somebody on the playground. A mean laugh.

This picture was drawn by: Alitzah Northrup Grade 4

Billy ran off stage and hid in the boys' restroom. He was never coming out.

A few minutes later Billy heard the door open and Mr. Answerpenny's voice, "Billy are you in here?"

"Yes," Billy answered, trying to hide his crying.

"I've come to see if you're alright."

"Yes," Billy said as he choked back a sob.

Mr. Answerpenny poked his head around the corner and looked at Billy. "Well, Mr. Fustertag, your parents are worried. I will tell them you're okay."

"But I'm not okay," Billy replied, "I didn't say anything."

"Why do you think that is, Billy?" asked Mr. Answerpenny.

"I don't know," said Billy. "Maybe I should have gone onstage first."

This picture was drawn by:
Melissa Toth
Grade 12

"Maybe, you should have practiced what you were going to say before the show," replied Mr. Answerpenny. "Being funny is a good gift to have, but performing is a skill that needs to be practiced. You never see a play that hasn't been practiced a hundred times before it's performed."

"Yeah, but I," Billy said and before he could finish his sentence Mr. Answerpenny spoke up.

"You are funny Billy. Telling jokes to your friends is using your natural talent, but getting onstage and doing a show takes hard work and preparation."

"Preparation?" Billy asked. He didn't think he knew what that word meant.

Mr. Answerpenny explained, "Preparation is when you figure out what you are going to do before you do it, and then practicing until you can do it without even thinking about it." Billy nodded his head like he understood.

This picture was drawn by: Kristen Baughn Grade 5

For the next couple of weeks Billy didn't feel very funny. No matter how much the other kids asked him, he would not do his jokes. No one spoke to Billy about his talent show fiasco, but he was sure they were giggling about it behind his back.

Mr. Answerpenny was as nice as ever, but Billy knew he was terribly disappointed. Billy was disappointed in himself, and he swore he would never do comedy again.

So, you can guess how surprised Billy Fustertag was when Mr. Answerpenny asked if he would perform his comedy in two weeks.

Mr. Answerpenny was organizing THE CITYWIDE BIG TALENT SHOWCASE TO BENEFIT PUPPY ADOPTION.

"Why would you want me?" Billy asked. "I messed up everything."

"You didn't mess up anything Billy," said Mr. Answerpenny. "The only person you let down, was Billy Fustertag.
I think you can do a great job, and I still don't have a comedian in the show."

This picture was drawn by: Kara Lambeck Grade 9

"But what if I get scared again and run away?" Billy asked already getting frightened.

"Well, Billy I'm willing to take the chance you won't, but you have to work with me really hard for an hour everyday after school until the night of the show. I've already talked to your parents, and they think it's a great idea."

Billy was scared, but Mr. Answerpenny, his mom, and dad wanted him to try.

"Uh," Billy was having trouble answering, "I guess I will do it."

"Great!" said Mr. Answerpenny. Billy thought Mr. Answerpenny was much too excited about Billy's chances of really being funny.

This picture was drawn by: Lacey Mehling Grade 5

For the next two weeks Billy worked very hard. Mr. Answerpenny said so. His mom and dad said they were very proud of how much time Billy had been practicing.

Billy's impressions never looked so sharp. His jokes were quick and funny. He worked on what order he was going to say everything until he could see his act in his sleep, but Billy was still frightened.

This picture was drawn by: Alicia Roos Grade 11

He didn't know "how frightened" until he was standing backstage at THE CITYWIDE BIG TALENT SHOWCASE TO BENEFIT PUPPY ADOPTION. The show was going on and Billy was next. He felt like he was too numb to move. Billy was now full of butterflies, which made him feel a little better, but not much.

Mr. Answerpenny went onstage and introduced Billy.
Billy couldn't move at first, but then forced himself to walk on the stage. He didn't run like before. Billy felt like he might fall down. When he reached the microphone in the middle of the stage, Billy looked at all the strange faces in the audience.

Then, Billy Fustertag started talking. He was very frightened but his comedy act was part of him now. He had prepared for so long and worked very hard he knew that no matter how many butterflies beat against his tummy, he could tell his stories and do his jokes.

Billy walked off the stage to thunderous applause. His parents stood up to clap, and he could see his mommy crying. She was crying happy tears like when Daddy bought her a new necklace for Christmas.

Mr. Answerpenny shook Billy's hand when he came backstage.

"That was terrific, Billy!" he exclaimed, and Billy started to smile. Billy was excited but no longer scared.

Billy now knew he was funny. And not only that, he knew he could do comedy in a real show in front of a real audience because he practiced.

Brad Tassell is a nationally known comedian and author who lives in Santa Claus, Indiana and was born on Halloween. He plays the ukulele and travels all over the country trying to get a smile.

Logan Sibrel was in the seventh grade when he was commissioned to draw the illustrations for this book. He is an extremely talented young man, and we are proud of his hard work and dedication to this project.

Other illustrations by:
Melissa Toth
Alitzah Northrup
Kristen Baughn
Lacey Mehling
Alicia Roos
Ashley Kamuf
Kara Lambeck
Alicia Ricklefs

Brad Tassell is available to schools across the USA. His show has great learning potential, helps students understand that they can succeed at any age, and induces a few laughs. Contact him at www.billyfustertag.com